Roc

SPACE TWINS

A Star is Born

Wendy Smith

A & C Black • London

Rockets series:

CROOK CATCHERS - Kar

HAUNTED MOUSE - Dee S

LITTLE T - Frank Rodger

MOTLEY'S CREW - Margaret Ryan & Margaret Chamberlain

MR CROC - Frank Rodgers

MRS MAGIC - Wendy Smith

MY FUNNY FAMILY - Colin West

ROVER - Chris Powling & Scoular Anderson

SILLY SAUSAGE - Michaela Morgan & Dee Shulman

SPACE TWINS - Wendy Smith

WIZARD'S BOY - Scoular Anderson

First paperback edition 2003
First published 2002 by A & C Black Publishers Ltd
37 Soho Square, London W1D 3QZ
www.acblack.com

ISBN 0-7136-6108-9

A CIP catalogue record for this book is available
from the British Library.

A & C Black uses paper produced with elemental
chlorine-free pulp, harvested from managed sustainable forests.

Printed and bound by G. Z. Printek, Bilbao, Spain.

Chapter One

Far away, on the other side of the
universe, flies the good ship Zazaza.

Each night it sends a signal.

Tonight, it's a full moon and the air is crisply clear.

Mik and Mak, the Space twins, are talking to Earth.

Down in East Volesey*, Wilbur Day
and his East Volesey Space Spotter Squad
are talking into space.

*a suburb on the fringe of nowhere.

After a bit of a time delay Wilbur
replied.

Mik and Mak did not understand.
In space, birthdays are not celebrated.
Time is quite a different matter on the
far side of the galaxy.

Mik and Mak could see that whatever it was, a birthday was an important day.

Chapter Two

Back down on Earth, Wilbur's mum and dad were having exactly the same problem.

And some of the East Volesey Space
Spotter Squad were also struggling
for ideas.

Ziggy pondered in the bath.

Ted was thinking on his morning walk.

Finally, they decided they would make
a new space-receiving kit.

Ziggy and Ted's idea
for an Alien Attracta.

Wilbur's mum thought it would be fun to take him on a shopping trip.

Wilbur was more worried
about getting
the bumps
at school.

ONE   TWO   THREE

He also
hoped he
had enough
pocket money
to stand a round
of cream cakes...

Mm

Do tuck
in.

Yum

And would he be having a party?

Mum and Dad haven't
said anything
about a party.

This problem was soon solved. The next morning, Grandma and Grandpa Day sent Wilbur a cheque through the post.

Wilbur read out the letter.

> ROSE COTTAGE
> WILLOWBANK
> WILTS
>
> Dear Wilbur –
> for our darling and only grandson, here is a cheque for £50 for your birthday party which we know you will be having soon.
> X X X
> Granma + Granpa   P S →

Wilbur wondered what the PS would be.

Wilbur didn't know whether to laugh or cry.

Chapter Three

Mik and Mak decided to see if Captain Lupo knew about birthdays.

He was busy planning the first
Inter-orbital Space Walk, when the cabin
door opened.

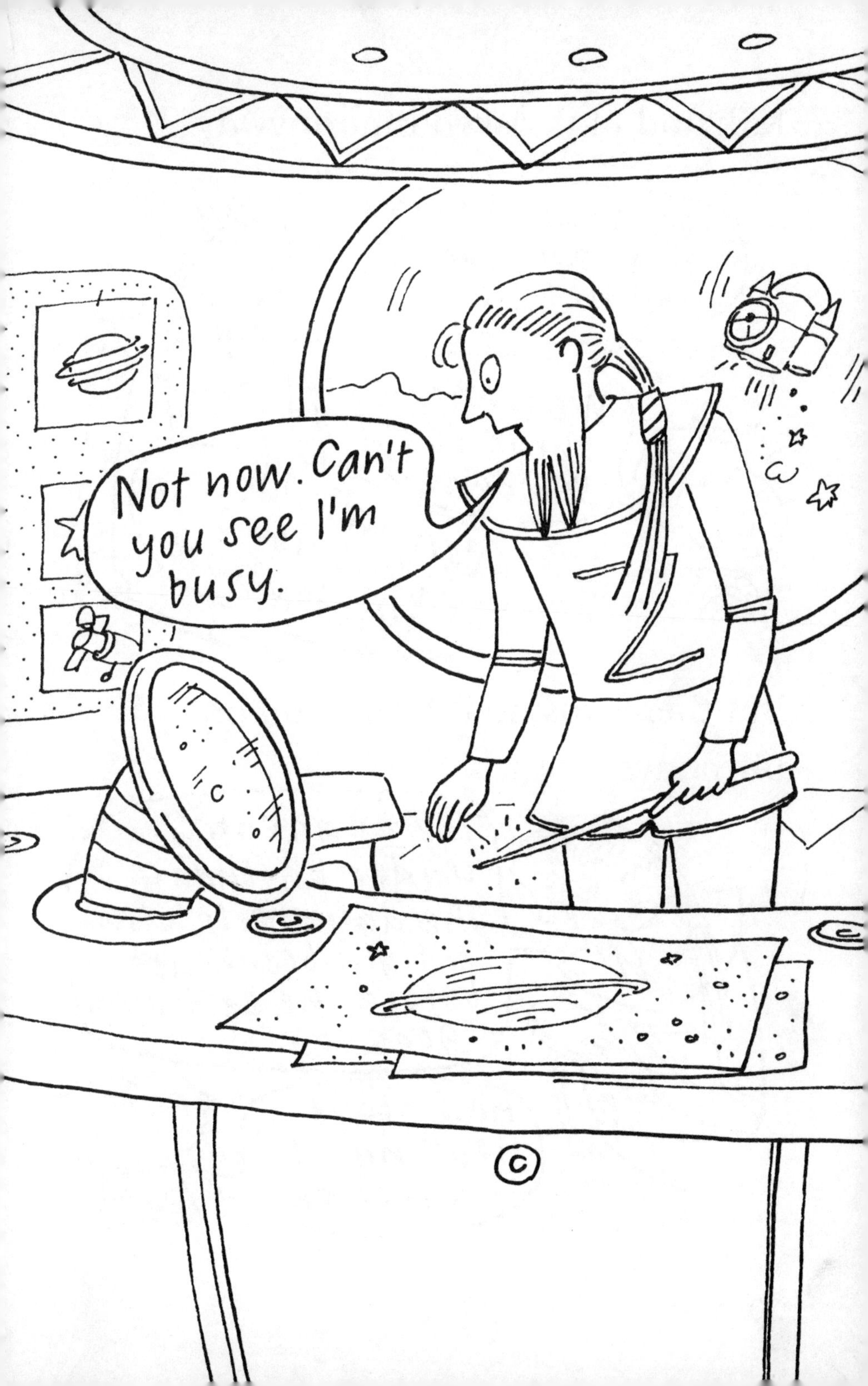
Not now. Can't you see I'm busy.

Mik and Mak asked him anyway.

But there was no information on birthdays.

Under 'surprise' there were two items.

Meteor Attack	Planetary Invasion
Meteor attacks are to be avoided. For further information consult the Orikal.	**In Venus** 3,000,000 light years past. Frog-like aliens stormed the capital, but were ejected by the Venusian Laysa force.

Captain Lupo remembered that Zuna had a gift catalogue.

Gift Catalogue

Cluster ring
22123

Star cluster set
In pure Venusiam for that special someone.

Crystal Balls
22124

Our crystals make you look even more gorgeous.

Anti-gravity glasses
22125

Always find your glasses rise to the sky? Not with our special nose-pin.

Beeper Keeper
22126

Keep your beeper where you want it, when you want it.

61

Mik and Mak didn't think these birthday surprises would be Wilbur's cup of tea*.

*There is no real equivalent in Spacespeak. The closest would be a beaker of Moondew.

But as luck would have it, when they went to make their Earth signal, an idea struck them both at the same time.

Wilbur was in no mood to talk to Mik and Mak that night. He had to give out the invitations to his party at the Maths Museum.

Ted and Ziggy were polite and accepted.

Chapter Four

As you might expect, the Maths
Museum party was not a popular idea.
Except with parents.

But no boy could be persuaded to go...

...and no girl either.

Which meant that in the end, the only people willing and able to go were the East Volesey Space Spotter Squad and Wilbur's mum and dad.

Wilbur's best friends worried that Wilbur wasn't going to have much fun.

So they were more than delighted when at last Mik and Mak got through on the eve of Wilbur's birthday.

Wilbur's message came through loud and clear. Captain Lupo gave Mik and Mak special permission to use his personal voicer.

Wilbur and the squad could barely sleep that night.

Just what were Mik and Mak up to?

Chapter Five

On the big day, Wilbur woke in a state of gloom.

There were lots of cards and presents.
Because of the Museum invitation lots of
people bought Wilbur maths presents.

All the while, Wilbur was wondering
how on earth he and the squad could
be on the roof at midnight.

It was Ziggy who came up with the idea.

Everyone set about making their dummies.

Ted suggested an emergency plan in case of trouble.

Wilbur thought of a secret code word.

And then off they all went to the
dreaded Maths Museum...

...which turned out to be more fun than Wilbur, Ted and Ziggy could ever have dreamed.

Chapter Six

Wilbur felt chuffed all the way home.
But the best was still to come.

At bedtime, Wilbur's mum and dad
had an extra little treat.

If Wilbur was watching TV with his parents, how could he get on the roof to talk with Mik and Mak?

Wilbur had not expected this at all.
He would have to put the emergency
plan into action.

Wilbur rang Ziggy using the secret code.

Ziggy rang Ted.

Mrs Day rang Ziggy's mum.

She rang Ted's mum.

Then Ted's mum rang Mrs Day.

Meanwhile, Wilbur and the squad
sneaked up onto the roof and waited.

Suddenly, the sky was filled with a stunning light show.

At the end of the show, Zuna and
Captain Lupo lit up their own present.
A new star named in Wilbur's honour.

Whenever he looks north, Wilbur sees his star twinkle, and imagines the Zazaza...

...which each night sends a signal.